for you to share special
with your grandchild

THE
Baby's
Lap Book

KAY CHORAO

Dutton Children's Books New York

Library of Congress Cataloging-in-Publication Data

Chorao, Kay.   The baby's lap book.
Summary: An anthology of familiar nursery rhymes.
1. Nursery rhymes. 2. Children's poetry.
[1. Nursery rhymes] 1. Title.
PZ8.3.C454Bab 1990   398.8   89-23273
ISBN 978-0-525-47330-5

Published in the United States by
Dutton Children's Books,
a division of Penguin Young Readers Group
345 Hudson Street, New York, New York 10014
www.penguin.com

Editor: Ann Durell   Designer: Riki Levinson
Manufactured in China
Revised Edition
7   9   10   8   6

This book belongs to

_____

Contents

This Little Pig

This little pig went to market,
This little pig stayed at home,
This little pig had roast beef,
This little pig had none,
And this little pig cried,
    Wee-wee, wee-wee,
All the way home.

Tickly, Tickly

Tickly, tickly, on your knee,
If you laugh, you don't love me.

Pat-A-Cake

Pat-a-cake, pat-a-cake, baker's man,
Bake me a cake as fast as you can;
Pat it and prick it, and mark it with B,
Put it in the oven for Baby and me.

Baa, Baa, Black Sheep

Baa, baa, black sheep,
    Have you any wool?
Yes, sir, yes, sir,
    Three bags full;
One for the master,
    And one for the dame,
And one for the little boy
    Who lives down the lane.

Little Boy Blue

Little boy blue,
    Come blow your horn,
The sheep's in the meadow,
    The cow's in the corn.

Where is the boy
    Who looks after the sheep?
He's under the haystack
    Fast asleep.

Will you wake him?
    No, not I.
For if I do,
    He's sure to cry.

Sing a Song of Sixpence

Sing a song of sixpence,
   A pocket full of rye;
Four and twenty blackbirds,
   Baked in a pie.

When the pie was opened,
   The birds began to sing;
Was not that a dainty dish,
   To set before a king?

The king was in his counting house,
   Counting out his money;
The queen was in the parlor,
   Eating bread and honey.
The maid was in the garden,
   Hanging out the clothes;
When down came a blackbird,
   And snipped off her nose.

Mary Had a Little Lamb

Mary had a little lamb,
   Its fleece was white as snow;
And everywhere that Mary went,
   The lamb was sure to go.
It followed her to school one day,
   That was against the rule;
It made the children laugh and play
   To see a lamb at school.

And so the teacher turned it out,
   But still it lingered near,
And waited patiently about
   Till Mary did appear.
"Why does the lamb love Mary so?"
   The eager children cry;
"Why, Mary loves the lamb, you know,"
   The teacher did reply.

Little Bo-Peep

Little Bo-Peep has lost her sheep,
And doesn't know where to find them;
Leave them alone, and they will come home,
Bringing their tails behind them.

Anna Maria

Anna Maria, she sat on the fire;

The fire was too hot, she sat on the pot;

The pot was too round, she sat on the ground;

The ground was too flat, she sat on the cat;

The cat ran away with Maria on her back.

Charley Barley

Charley Barley, butter and eggs,
Sold his wife for three duck eggs.
When the ducks began to lay,
Charley Barley flew away.

Old King Cole

Old King Cole
Was a merry old soul,
And a merry old soul was he;

He called for his pipe,
And he called for his bowl,
And he called for his fiddlers three.

Every fiddler, he had a fiddle,
And a very fine fiddle had he;
Oh, there's none so rare
As can compare
With King Cole and his fiddlers three.

Willie Winkie

Wee Willie Winkie   Rapping at the window,
     Runs through the town,   Crying through the lock,
Upstairs and downstairs   "Are the children all in bed?
     In his nightgown,   For now it's eight o'clock."

Goosey Gander

Goosey, goosey, gander,
   Where do you wander?
Upstairs and downstairs
   And in my lady's chamber.

There I met an old man
   Who would not say his prayers,
I took him by the left leg
   And threw him down the stairs.

It's Raining, It's Pouring

It's raining, it's pouring,
The old man's snoring,
He got into bed
And bumped his head
And couldn't get up in the morning.

Doctor Foster

Doctor Foster went to Gloucester,
In a shower of rain;
He stepped in a puddle,
Right up to his middle,
And never went there again.

Little Miss Muffet

Little Miss Muffet
Sat on a tuffet,
  Eating her curds and whey;
There came a big spider,
Who sat down beside her,
  And frightened Miss Muffet away.

Jack Horner

Little Jack Horner
Sat in the corner,
Eating his Christmas pie;
He put in his thumb,
And pulled out a plum,
And said,
 "What a good boy am I!"

Tom Tinker's Dog

Bow, wow, wow,
Whose dog art thou?
Little Tom Tinker's dog,
Bow, wow, wow.

Where Has My Little Dog Gone?

Oh where, oh where has my little dog gone?
Oh where, oh where can he be?
With his ears cut short and his tail cut long,
Oh where, oh where is he?

Old Mother Hubbard

Old Mother Hubbard
Went to the cupboard
To fetch her poor dog a bone,
But when she got there
The cupboard was bare
And so the poor dog had none.

Three Men in a Tub

Rub-a-dub-dub,

Three men in a tub,

And how do you think they be?

The butcher, the baker,

The candlestick maker,

They all jumped out of a rotten potato!

Turn them out, knaves all three!

Cobbler, Cobbler

Cobbler, cobbler, mend my shoe,
Get it done by half-past two;
Half-past two is far too late,
Get it done by half-past eight.

The Old Woman in a Shoe

There was an old woman who lived in a shoe,
She had so many children, she didn't know what to do;
She gave them some broth without any bread,
She whipped them all soundly and put them to bed.

The Cat and the Fiddle

Hey diddle, diddle,

The cat and the fiddle,

The cow jumped over the moon;

The little dog laughed

To see such sport,

And the dish ran away with the spoon.

The Three Little Kittens

Three little kittens
They lost their mittens,
   And they began to cry,
Oh, Mother dear, we sadly fear
   Our mittens we have lost.

What! Lost your mittens,
You naughty kittens!
Then you shall have no pie.
Mee-ow, mee-ow, mee-ow,
No, you shall have no pie.

Jack and Jill

Jack and Jill
Went up the hill,
To fetch a pail of water;
Jack fell down,
And broke his crown,
And Jill came tumbling after.

Then up Jack got,
And home did trot,
As fast as he could caper;
Went to bed
And bound his head
With vinegar and brown paper.

Diddle, Diddle, Dumpling

Diddle, diddle, dumpling, my son John,
Went to bed with his trousers on;
One shoe off, and one shoe on,
Diddle, diddle, dumpling, my son John.

Hickory, Dickory, Dock

Hickory, dickory, dock,
The mouse ran up the clock,
The clock struck one,
The mouse ran down,
Hickory, dickory, dock.

Three Blind Mice

Three blind mice, see how they run!
They all ran after the farmer's wife,
Who cut off their tails with a carving knife,
Did you ever see such a thing in your life,
As three blind mice?

Humpty Dumpty

Humpty Dumpty sat on a wall,
Humpty Dumpty had a great fall.
All the King's horses and all the King's men
Couldn't put Humpty together again.

Peter, Pumpkin Eater

Peter, Peter, pumpkin eater,
Had a wife and couldn't keep her;
He put her in a pumpkin shell,
And there he kept her very well.

Lucy Locket

Lucy Locket
Lost her pocket.
Kitty Fisher found it!
But not a penny
Was there in it
Except the ribbon round it.

A Crooked Man

There was a crooked man,
    And he went a crooked mile;
He found a crooked sixpence
    Against a crooked stile;
He bought a crooked cat,
    Which caught a crooked mouse;
And they all lived together
    In a little crooked house.

What Will Poor Robin Do?

The north wind doth blow,

And we shall have snow,

And what will poor Robin do then?

    Poor thing!

He'll sit in a barn,

And keep himself warm,

And hide his head under his wing,

    Poor thing!

Poll Parrot

Little Poll Parrot

Sat in his garret

    Eating toast and tea;

A little brown mouse

Jumped into the house

    And stole it all away.

Barber, Barber

Barber, barber, shave a pig,
How many hairs will make a wig?
"Four and twenty, that's enough."
Give the barber a pinch of snuff.

Tom, the Piper's Son

Tom, Tom, the piper's son,

Stole a pig and away he run;

    The pig was eat

    And Tom was beat,

And Tom went howling down the street.

Jumping Joan

Here am I,
    Little Jumping Joan;
When nobody's with me
I'm all alone.

Jack Be Nimble

Jack be nimble,
Jack be quick,
Jack jump over
The candlestick.

Jerry Hall

Jerry Hall,
He is so small,
A rat could eat him,
Hat and all.

Pussy's in the Well

Ding, dong, bell,
Pussy's in the well.

Who put her in?   What a naughty boy was that
Little Johnny Green.   To try to drown poor pussy cat,
Who pulled her out?   Who never did him any harm
Little Tommy Stout.   And killed the mice in his father's barn.

Pussy Cat

Pussy cat, pussy cat,
    Where have you been?
I've been to London
    To look at the Queen.
Pussy cat, pussy cat,
    What did you there?
I frightened a little mouse
    Under her chair.

The Way the Ladies Ride

This is the way the ladies ride,
  Tri, tre, tre, tree,
  Tri, tre, tre, tree!
This is the way the gentlemen ride,
  Gallop-a-trot,
  Gallop-a-trot!
This is the way the farmers ride,
  Hobbledy-hoy,
  Hobbledy-hoy!

Ride a Cock-Horse

Ride a cock-horse to Banbury Cross,
To see a fine lady upon a white horse.
Rings on her fingers and bells on her toes,
And she shall have music wherever she goes.

My Black Hen

Hickety, pickety, my black hen,
She lays eggs for gentlemen.
Gentlemen come every day
To see what my black hen doth lay.

The Little Nut Tree

I had a little nut tree,
    Nothing would it bear
But a silver nutmeg,
    And a golden pear;

The King of Spain's daughter
    Came to visit me,
And all for the sake
    Of my little nut tree.

Little Girl With a Curl

There was a little girl,
And she had a little curl
Right in the middle of her forehead;
When she was good, she was very, very good,
But when she was bad, she was horrid.

Contrary Mary

Mary, Mary, quite contrary,
How does your garden grow?
With silver bells and cockle shells,
And pretty maids all in a row.

Tweedledum and Tweedledee

Tweedledum and Tweedledee
　　Agreed to have a battle,
For Tweedledum said Tweedledee
　　Had spoiled his nice new rattle.

Just then flew by a monstrous crow
　　As big as a tar barrel,
Which frightened both the heroes so,
　　They quite forgot their quarrel.

Georgie Porgie

Georgie Porgie, pudding and pie,
Kissed the girls and made them cry;
When the boys came out to play,
Georgie Porgie ran away.

Twinkle, Little Star

Twinkle, twinkle, little star,
How I wonder what you are!
Up above the world so high,
Like a diamond in the sky.

Old Woman Tossed Up in a Basket

There was an old woman tossed up in a basket,
Seventeen times as high as the moon;
Where she was going I couldn't but ask it,
For in her hand she carried a broom.
"Old woman, old woman, old woman," said I,
"Where are you going to, up so high?"
"To brush the cobwebs off the sky!"
"May I go with you?" "Aye, by and by."

Baby Bye

Baby Bye, here's a fly
We must watch him
   You and I.
There he goes
On his toes,
Over Baby's nose.

Goose Feathers

Cackle, cackle, Mother Goose,
Have you any feathers loose?
Truly have I, pretty fellow,
Half enough to fill a pillow.
Here are quills, take one or two,
And down to make a bed for you.

Derry, Down Derry

Derry, down derry, and up in the air,
Baby shall ride without pony or mare,
Clasped in my arms like a queen on a throne,
Prettiest rider that ever was known.

Little Polly Flinders

Little Polly Flinders
Sat among the cinders,
    Warming her pretty little toes.
Her mother came and caught her,
And smacked her little daughter
    For spoiling her nice new clothes.

Rock-A-Bye Baby

Rock-a-bye, baby,
On the tree top,
When the wind blows
The cradle will rock;
When the bough breaks
The cradle will fall,
And down will come baby,
Cradle and all.

Rabbit Skin

Bye, baby bunting,
Daddy's gone a-hunting,
Gone to get a rabbit skin
To wrap the baby bunting in.